Wave Goodbye at the Corner

MW00413624

By

Thomas C. Green

Compiled and Edited by Tim Green and Norma Green Heath
Cover art and story and poetry illustrations by Judy Madren

If you like this book and think it is
Worthwhile- please make a post to
your Facebook.
Feedback welcomed
tdgreen02@bellsouth.net

Thank you
Tim Green

ISBN-13:978-1799056621
Printing Platform: KDP.Amazon.com

INTRODUCTION

Thomas Claude Green was born in 1909 near Atlanta, Georgia. He grew up with two older brothers and his parents on  a tenant farm. School terms evolved around a cotton economy – in session six months during the winter and in recess for six months during the planting, growing and harvesting season.

Dad remembered making rhymes as early as age nine. When he was twelve years old, his mother bought a guitar for him and within two years he was writing and singing his own songs.

In January, 1924, at age 14, Dad surrendered his youth, taking a job in a cotton mill working 60+ hours per week to help support his family financially. Like his limited formal education opportunities, his boyhood pursuits were also limited: fishing in the nearby pond, wading in the 'crick', chasing frogs or tadpoles, and taking barefoot excursions through forest and fields. I'm sure he missed fulfilling his passion and favorite pastime of playing baseball in the cow pasture. His story, "Wave Goodbye at the Corner", captures and portrays many everlasting heartfelt moments and times with his family and reveals how laboring in the cotton mill under grueling conditions transformed him for decades to come. He saw firsthand on a daily basis his mother's losing battle with cancer.

He realized full well the adversity his father faced during harsh economic times and he came to understand that the ability to survive oftentimes depended on one's ability to produce – no unemployment insurance, no social security. These momentous experiences were pivotal and ushered Dad, somewhat callously, from boyhood to manhood.

Dad's early working career was largely in textiles, including Dunean Mill in Greenville, S.C. and Gaston and Alamance Counties in N.C. During World War II he worked in a military airplane factory. He also held miscellaneous jobs until the late

1950's when he began work in a cabinet shop. Locating in Greensboro, N.C., he continued working until and after retirement in cabinet manufacturing.

Dad's hobbies included flower and vegetable gardening, stained glass creations, various wood working projects, and maybe his biggest challenge was that of building a clock with all parts and movements he made of wood. Dad loved to spend time with his cats whether indoors or out inspiring "My Tom Cat" and "My Four Cats". He was a voracious reader of novels – among his favorites were *Grapes of Wrath* and Zane Grey westerns.

Dad was very proud to have been a member of the Masonic Lodge organization for more than 55 years becoming a Master Mason and advancing to the 32nd degree.

A favorite past time was writing songs and playing them on the guitar for family and friends when they came to visit. A bonus would be to hear Dad's latest tall tale or funny story which he would tell with a straight face and then laugh with you as if he had never heard it before. He would rather tell a funny story than eat when he was hungry.

One can easily trace Dad's life journey through his writings spanning ages 9 to 89. They are akin to a kaleidoscope of frequently changing, colorful and wide-ranging subjects reflecting early childhood remembrances, intense pride in community and country, and a strong sense of empathy and caring for his fellow man. He was greatly troubled by environmental threats, pollution and the negative impact on nature and society. His short stories and poems describing early childhood are heavily influenced by actual occurrences substantiated by documented records and Dad's own recollections consistent with a relative's account, although it's hard to deny there may have been slight embellishments along the way.

"Big Moon" is so reflective of a frequent subject of Dad's – his thoughts about romance and love – puppy love, forsaken love and pursuit of lasting love. Low points in Dad's life became some of his most prolific. In "I Remember" Dad wrote, "I could write a book of them (memories), one at a time. When I think of one, there is one close behind." Dad said years ago he "had to put down all these things because I have to… I have to get 'em out… get 'em out of my head and the only way to do that was to write 'em down, otherwise they would worry me to death." He kept a pad and pencil at his bedside to record immediate thoughts to be completed later.

Dad was a devout Christian and lived his faith daily. Such was the focus of numerous writings. Typically, two or three nights a week he would devotedly study the Bible and related books preparing notes on a pad for the Adult Sunday School class he taught for more than twenty years at Kinnett Memorial Baptist Church in Burlington, N.C. He was a most humble and thankful person. It has been said truly thankful people rarely have a bad attitude. Dad was no exception. Even as a single parent he was always upbeat.

Dad's sense of humor was ever-present and he could easily find humor in the most mundane circumstances. The two things most important to Dad were his faith and his family. He lived simply and demonstrated a Trojan work ethic all his life, but he fell short of enjoying much financial success; however, his riches were clearly conveyed in a writing…"I Wouldn't Give a Nickel for my Future but 'I Wouldn't Take a Million for my Memories'". It is not unusual for someone having read Dad's writings to say, "I feel like I knew him or I wish I had met him." He passed away at age 95 in 2005.

We appreciate your interest in the writings of our Dad. We hope you will find a favorite within and share it with a friend.

DEDICATION

WAVE GOODBYE AT THE CORNER
is
dedicated to the memory of our Dad and the many gifts
he gave us including an unshakeable eternal faith
and a wit and humor like none other.

CONTENTS

PART I: SHORT STORIES

WAVE GOODBYE AT THE CORNER

I went to bed early that cold Sunday night, January 1924. I pulled the covers over me and lay there shivering for a long time before I could get warm enough to relax. I knew I would have to get up at five the next morning and be in the mill by six. My dad had asked his boss at the mill to give me a job. I had just passed my 14th birthday and knew now that my school days were over. I wondered what kind of work I'd do and how much money I'd make.

My dad didn't make enough to pay the bills although he worked every day. Maybe the money that I would make would help out. With all these thoughts passing through my mind, sleep caught up with me. The next sound I heard was the five o'clock wake whistle. The low mournful sound seemed to hold me suspended in space as it grew louder and louder until it woke me; then silence. About 30 seconds later the whistle came again, low and mournful. I didn't know it then but for the next seven years I would eat, sleep, and work by the sound of that whistle. The only time we didn't hear it was Sundays.

I heard my dad in the next room shaking the clinkers out of the coal grate in the fireplace. Although I couldn't see him I knew by the sound of rattling newspaper that he was getting a fire going. I heard him break the kindling, then the coal bucket rattled and the striking of a match. I heard him come from the bedroom to the kitchen and strike a match to light the four burner oil stove. He rinsed out the coffee pot, put it on the stove, went back to the bedroom and said something to my mother. I was almost asleep when I heard Mama come into the kitchen a few minutes later and heard her put the biscuits in the oven.

Dad came to my door then and said, "Son, you'd better get up. Breakfast is nearly ready. You don't want to be late your first day in the mill."

I lay there for another minute dreading to get up. It was one of those blue cold mornings. The floor felt like ice to my feet. I grabbed my clothes and shoes and ran into the bedroom where dad had the fire going. I put my overalls on along with a blue chamby work shirt and socks and shoes and went into the kitchen to the wash table set off on the side, washed the sleep from my eyes, put some cold water on my hair to make it stay down, combed it and sat down.

I took a biscuit and broke it open, poured some black molasses on it, ate it and drank a cup of black coffee. I pulled on my blue denim jacket and an old mill cap. Pulling the collar up and the cap down, I started for the door. Dad was sipping coffee at the table. He called to me and said, "Son, do your best on the job. Do what your boss tells you to do. Treat him right and he will treat you right." I said, "Dad, I will do my best" and turned toward the door. Dad kept on sipping his coffee.

Mama followed me to the door and pulled my jacket collar a little higher. I opened the door and went out. It was still dark except for the sky in the east. I walked toward the corner and just as I went around the corner I glanced back. My mother was outlined in the front door. I waved goodbye at the corner, pushed my hands deep in my pockets, hunched my shoulders against the cold and walked faster and faster toward the mill.

Tears ran down my face. I knew at that moment I was walking away from boyhood too soon, turning into a man too soon. When I got to the mill I was running, afraid to slow down to a walk. I might be tempted to turn around and go back home. My dad told me to go all the way past the spinning department to a big door on the right—it was so big I could hardly push it open. I went in; the steam heat seemed to crawl all over my cold body and I felt like going to sleep standing up. Two women were in the hallway hanging up their coats in a long row of cupboards. I put my jacket and cap on a nail and went in search of the overseer.

A woman operating a machine told me that he was in the office. I went in and told him who I was and he said my dad had talked to him about my going to work. He took me to the section man where several people were standing around waiting for the night shift to quit work at six. In five minutes I would start working my first day in the cotton mill. The hours from 6 to 12 were long and dragged on and on. From 12 to 1 we went to lunch. The steam heat and the labor we put into the work made sweat run down our faces.

Even on the coldest days our clothes would get wringing wet even with the doors and windows open. In the summertime, inside was almost unbearable. The heat and lint dust, the odor of hot motors and the scent of our own bodies was sickening. Two years after my first day in the mill an opening came on the night shift. I asked for the job and got it.

At 16, I would have the full responsibility of the job. I had learned a lot in two years. The next five years put terrific pressure on me. Production had to be maintained, machines had to be fixed, personnel problems had to be solved, reports and time sheets had to be kept up to date. All this in my growing years stunted me but I grew lean and tall. When I had time I studied cotton mill math and began to realize that I really did like cotton mill work. I liked to hear the humming of the spindles, the slap of the picker stick when it put the shuttle back and forth in the loom with the speed of a bullet.

The odor of sweating bodies, the smell of hot motors, the flying lint and problems didn't bother me too much. I took them all in stride. Each night was a challenge and I met all of them head on.

Seven years now I had waved goodbye at the corner to my mother. In the winter months I could just barely see her against the light in the background standing in the door. In the summer months she'd be sitting on the porch. As I turned the corner she'd wave and I'd wave back.

I came home from work one morning in 1930 and dad said that Mama was sick and had to see a doctor. I asked him what was wrong but he didn't tell me at the time. After several trips to the doctor, I asked my mother what was wrong. She didn't want to tell me but I insisted. Then she said the doctor thought she had cancer. I was so shocked I could hardly believe it. A few days later she was taken to the hospital. When I would leave the house for work I'd turn to look back.

From the corner I raised my hand to wave. For an instant I could almost see Mama standing in the door. Tears ran down my face just like they did on that cold January morning in 1924 (the first day I went to work in the mill).

Mama came home from the hospital after several weeks and seemed to be gaining some of the strength back that she had lost. For about a year Mama was able to live a normal life. Almost without warning Mama was ill again.

When the doctors operated the year before they failed to get all of the cancer. Now it was in another part of her body. Once again she was taken to the hospital. I noticed my dad's face was old and tired. He had a hard job in the mill and the strain of Mama's illness was too much for him. Mama was brought home from the hospital. We were told by the doctors that all had been done that could be done. It was just a matter of time now.

The months that followed were like a nightmare for me as I watched my mother die a little each day. I would come home from work and find her awake and knew that she had not slept, yet the smile that greeted me each morning was the same. She never complained and always asked about my work. I never worried her with my problems. I would go to my room and try to sleep. It was impossible to do my work without sleep. It was hard to fall asleep wondering if Mama would last through the day.

Then one morning I came home from work and Mama was in a coma. Between 10 and 11 that morning she passed away.

The family came home from the funeral to a dark and lonely house. I saw the grief on my Dad's face and tears choked the words in his throat when he tried to speak. My two brothers were stricken with grief and my heart was about to burst because I couldn't cry. I would cry tonight in the darkness of my room and tomorrow I would cry and the day after and the day after that. I believe that when my eyes shall close in death, there will be tears of grief under the lids.

Dad and I tried to drown our grief in our work. He worked the day shift and I continued to work at night. Several months after my mother's death, dad began to show signs of being unable to do a day's work. My mother's death, the hard work in the mill and his age brought about the decision to sell the furniture and dad would live with my older brother. I would get a place to board with a friend in the mill village. We sold most of the furniture and gave some away until we emptied the house because it belonged to the mill. I had to tell them at the office that it was empty. Dad had already gone and I had made sure that nothing was left in the house. Already I had decided that I would just walk out and not look back. I got almost through the door; then I had an urge to take just one last look. I went back into my room and memories flooded my soul and I remembered the times I had stayed in this room. I had read books into the midnight hours and these books carried me to just about every part of the world. When I would become tired of reading I would drop off to sleep.

The happiest hours of my life were spent in this room and when I left it I would leave a part of myself there. I went into the kitchen. I could almost see my mother kneading the dough for the breakfast biscuits. I remembered the times when the family would come together and all the good food that Mama prepared for their coming. I remembered the good times when we sat around the table and talked, ate and laughed. I went into the bedroom where Mama and dad had slept. The fireplace was in this room and winter nights we'd sit around the small coal grate until the fire slowly died out.

I wondered how many tears had been shed in this room, how many nights had they laid and worried about the bills, and how many times had they worried about me. I remembered their love for each other and their love for me. I counted myself fortunate to have had such a mom and dad. From my childhood to this moment, if a price could be put on that part of my life, there is not enough money in the world to buy this from me.

I walked out, locked the front door, dropped the key in my pocket and walked down the street toward the corner. I turned at the corner and glanced back at the old house and for one brief moment I could almost see my mother standing in the door. I raised my arm to wave but caught myself and let it fall at my side and walked fast toward the place where I was to live with a friend.

CHURCH PICNIC WITH MY NEW SHOES

The fourth Sunday in June at the Baptist Church was an all day affair. By 8 o'clock, under every shade tree, there was a buggy, one horse wagon or a two horse wagon. They came from miles around; children in their Sunday best, old people, middle-aged, teenagers and babies in diapers. The singing started about 10 o'clock and they raised the roof 'til about 11:30.

Then the preacher started his sermon which lasted at least 1 ½ hours. He preached hell fire and damnation for the sinner and heavenly paradise for the saved. My dad had somehow managed to buy me a new pair of shoes on Saturday before this fourth Sunday in June. I dressed in my knee pants and long ribbed black stockings and, with a lot of misgiving and pushing, I put those shoes on, buttoned them up and walked around a lot looking down with pride at my new shoes.

Mama put the basket of fried chicken, homemade cakes and pies in the buggy. We all piled in and headed for the church and got there about 9 o'clock. I strutted around outside the church so everybody could see my new shoes. The sun was really hot that day. I think it tried to melt everybody and everything. By the time we'd gotten into the church and settled down, every seat was taken and people were standing around the walls and down the aisles. The heat from the closely packed congregation and the heat from outside made the inside of the church as hot as an oven. It didn't take long for the heat to get to me.

My new shoes began to tighten up and my feet began to burn like somebody had given me the hot foot. About the time the preacher was half through his sermon I couldn't stand the burning any longer and figured everybody was looking at the preacher so I unbuttoned my shoes and slipped them off under the pew. He preached about another hour.

After he ended the sermon he began to praise all the good women of the church on how they had spent many hours in the kitchen on Saturday preparing all the good food out there in those buggies and wagons. After the preacher finished talking about the fried chicken and homemade cakes and pies, they sang a hymn and had the benediction and everybody got ready to go outside.

Mama said, "Let's go" and she kept trying to get me to stand up.

I said, "I can't go out there."

She said, "Why?" I said, "Mama, I took off my shoes. Now my feet are swollen and I can't get them on again." Mama looked at me as if she was disgusted with the whole world.

She said, "Take off your stockings, put them in your shoes and come on." We went outside. After having about six of my toes stepped on by people in a hurry to get to the food on the long table under the shade trees, I thought everybody there was looking at my red swollen feet. But now when I think about all the food that was consumed and all the people moving around, I doubt if anybody noticed my feet.

I was scared to death all the time I was trying to eat. I was kept busy trying to keep people from stepping on my red swollen feet. After about a couple of hours around the table, everybody got ready to go back into the church for some more singing. I noticed that the singing was slightly off key and somewhat lower in volume than in the morning hours due to the fact that too much fried chicken and homemade cake and pie had caused many of the singers to have shortness of breath. Late in the afternoon the singing broke up.

People began to say goodbye and started hitching up for the ride home. Dresses were wrinkled, collars were wilted and babies were crying because they hadn't been changed often enough. When the goodbyes were said they talked about what a good day it had been. We had to eat leftovers for supper that night. I had a chicken wing, a biscuit and a piece of cake that somebody had eaten part of and put back on the plate. I don't know whatever happened to those shoes. I tried to bury them in the cornfield but my dad caught me and threatened to make me wear them anyway.

Even now when I see a kid with shoes on in the summertime I wonder if they are hurting his feet. Now 52 years later (1971), every time I think of those shoes, my feet start hurting.

BAPTIZING THE HOUNDS

My cousin, Lester, his sister, Hester, and I were five years old (1914). We played together until we were ten. All of Lester's family were Methodist and all of my family were Baptist. In Lester's yard was a long grape arbor and when the grapevine leaves were full grown, they completely covered the arbor.

This made it an almost perfect place for us kids to play. Lester had vowed since the day he could talk that he would someday be a Methodist preacher. Hester always wanted to play the organ. Lester decided that the grape arbor would be a good place to play church. We usually had three or four hound dogs at our house down the road about a quarter of a mile. Lester had four mixed breed dogs. Most of the time in hot weather these dogs just laid around in the shade and slept. Once in a while they'd wake up and snap at the flies that bothered them. They were supposed to be rabbit dogs but I doubt if half of the whole pack ever saw a rabbit much less smelled one long enough to trail it. About the only thing they could catch was a biscuit. I'd pitch biscuits out the back door to any one of the hounds and they never missed. I pitched a pod of boiled okra to one and he caught it and it slipped down his throat so fast that he started looking for it. He ran around the back yard for two hours hunting that pod of okra.

One day Lester had a bright idea. He gathered all the dogs and had them lay down under the grape arbor, got two rocks and made Hester an organ, found a box and made a pulpit. Then we all gathered there and Lester crawled on that box and began to preach. All the dogs slept through the sermon.

Then Hester played the make believe organ and sang "Jesus, Lover of my Soul". I think this one song was the only one she knew. At least that's the only one I ever heard her sing. Then Lester had another bright idea -- he said he believed the dogs had heard enough of his sermons to be converted so he got a glass of water and baptized them by sprinkling water on their heads. The dogs seemed to enjoy the sprinkling; it cooled them off some anyway. This sprinkling and preaching went on for a week or two and then I got a bright idea. I told Lester that I believed those dogs had about enough of sprinkling and I thought that they should be converted to Baptist and at the end of his sermon I thought they should be taken to the creek and baptized.

At the end of the sermon Hester sang "Jesus, Lover of my Soul". We managed to carry, pull and drag those hound dogs to the creek and baptized them every day for about two weeks. I was so worn out dragging those hound dogs to the creek and dipping them under that I decided this was enough.

Lester said he believed that now we had eight converted dogs and I said, "Converted to what? We've sprinkled and baptized so much that now they are so confused they don't know whether they are Methodist or Baptist." Now 52 years later, I wonder if any of those dogs ever made it into dog heaven.

WILD BUGGY RIDE

My dad told my brother and me, on a Friday night, that if we could get caught up with the plowing by three or four o'clock the next day, we could go into town. We were in the field by sun up and by four o'clock that afternoon we had finished the plowing and headed for the barn. We watered the mules, rubbed the mare down so she'd be ready to go, cleaned up and put on our clean overalls, hitched the mare to the buggy and headed for town.

We walked up and down the main street about 10 times looking in the store windows. I had a quarter I'd been saving. I stopped in front of a store and a man was inside putting pieces of bread on his arm. He had the bread split open, put the wieners in the bread and then smeared what looked like yellow grease on them with a wooden paddle. The sign said "Hog Dogs 5 cents". I could smell what he was fixing—sure smelled good. I wish I could have inhaled four or five of them and saved my quarter.

I went in and ordered one and a Nu-Grape drink. After the first one, the man kept on 'til he'd sold me three more. I gave him the quarter and went on down the street where I found my brother standing in front of the feed store eating a raw sweet potato. I didn't tell him I was so full of hot dogs I could hardly breathe. By the time we'd walked up and down the main street seven or eight more times it began to get dark. My brother said it was time we headed for home.

We got in the buggy and were almost out of town where about two miles of the smooth dirt road ran alongside the railroad tracks.

A fast freight train came up from behind and just as the engine got even with the buggy, the engineer sorta grinned, reached up and got that whistle cord and the whistle let out a blast that nearly busted my eardrums. That mare crossed her ears and started to run.

My brother braced his feet against the floor boards and tried to hold her, but she had the bit in her teeth and she kept right alongside that engine. About every quarter mile that engineer got hold of that whistle cord, grinned and almost blasted us out of the buggy. That mare got faster and faster. I started to jump but I couldn't turn loose long enough to try it. Just before we got to the turn off, that engineer gave that whistle one more pull and headed for Birmingham. We made the turn on two wheels, one in front, one behind and when we hit the rough road we were making about twenty miles per hour—five on the road and fifteen up and down. It was 1 ½ miles from the turn off to our house. The rough road slowed the mare down some but she still had the bit in her teeth when we passed my uncle's house.

He said later, "That buggy was raising so much dust he thought one of those Texas dust storms had got loose and headed up through Georgia." We made the turn into the yard at the house alright, but that fool mare didn't start putting on brakes 'til she got within five feet of the corn crib. The buggy came to a screeching halt and I piled out. My legs were so weak I could hardly walk. It's a good thing I ate all those hot dogs; I wouldn't have had the strength to walk to the house. Now 52 years later, every time I hear a train whistle I am reminded of that wild ride on a Saturday night in Georgia. I wonder why they didn't have brakes put on buggies.

HALFWAY TO THE GRAVEYARD

My Grandfather had been dead now for over a year (1919). Every Saturday since his death my mother, her sister, my two cousins and I made the trip to the graveyard to clean off his grave and put fresh flowers on it. Usually most of the men folk worked in the fields or went to town on Saturday afternoons. I always dreaded for Saturday to come—I'd have to take a bath and go to the graveyard. I'd thought about it a lot and decided that I wasn't going anymore. Mama had already called five or six times. I was hiding under the house. The two hound dogs were under there and had dug holes trying to find a cool place.

Every once in a while they'd wake up long enough to snap at a fly. I heard Mama come down the back steps and I peeped out to see where she was headed and when she headed for the peach tree in the back yard and reached up for a limb, I figured it was time for me to make a move. I headed for the back porch but didn't quite make it. Mama caught me by the seat of my pants and warned me if I didn't get in that back room and get in that wash tub I'd get a big dose of peach tree tea. I'd had several doses of that recently; once for trying to throw the cat in the well and once for tying a tin can to the dog's tail. After I'd scrubbed the dirt off and soaked some of the rust off my feet I got ready to dress. I noticed my brother's Sunday shirt hanging on a nail and the hard starched collar that went with it. (The kind that is fastened in the back on the band of the shirt with a collar button. Another collar button holds the two ends together in front.) I worked with it until I finally got it on, then I put on my overalls and yelled to Mama that I was ready to go. She went out on the front porch and hollered like a wild Indian. Her sister must have heard her about a quarter of a mile up the dirt road. In just a minute I

saw my aunt and two cousins running down the dusty road. The things (rake, hoe, jar of water, brush broom, and an arm load of flowers) we had to carry over there every Saturday would fill a one horse wagon. I sorta hung back 'til everybody started down the road. I walked slow following them, afraid the shock my mother would get when she spotted my brother's shirt and collar would be too much for her.

We got about half way to the graveyard (I was sweating like a hog in a fur coat) when that hard starched collar came unbuttoned in front and popped like a rifle shot. My mother stopped, turned around and when she saw that collar still fastened in the back sticking straight out on each side of my head like airplane wings, she let out a yell like a wild Indian and said, "What in God's name are you doing with your brother's Sunday shirt on?" I didn't see any peach trees alongside the road, but there were plenty of black gum bushes. Mama broke one off and I ate supper that night standing up. Now 52 years later every time I

hear a rifle shot or a car backfire, I am reminded of that hard starched collar and a hot Saturday afternoon in Georgia when I just got halfway to the graveyard.

PART II.   POEMS HUMOR

A STORMY NIGHT IN THE COUNTRY

Old farm house sitting low on the ground;
Every time it thundered something fell down.
Holes in the roof, cracks in the floor,
Windows falling out, can't close the door

The wind blew hard; we had a bad storm.
Blew the roof from the old hay barn
Rained all night, rained all day;
Drowned the hogs and ruined the hay

The rain came in through the holes in the roof.
Water ran out through the cracks in the floor.
Mama's cooking cornbread and black-eyed peas.
The wind blew her nightgown up in the trees.

The lightning flashed, the thunder boomed,
Shook the walls in every room.
Grandpa's picture came down end over end.
Lightning struck the old hog pen.

Papa said the storm has let up a bit.
Grandma's picture ain't fell down yet.
Mama's still cooking, the wood is all wet.
She said, "It ain't rained on the cornbread yet."
Yonder comes the preacher with that Bible of his.
He talks about the Promised Land but he don't know where
it is.

He talks about the creation and when the world began
And said Jesus is coming but he don't know when.

We had a bad night in the country. The storm took its toll –
Coffee in the coffee pot, gravy in the bowl.
Papa said the blessing. This is what he said,
"God bless America and please pass the cornbread."

ARTHRITIS

I'm hurting all over and have shortness of breath.
This old arthritis is gonna put me to death.
I'm popping pain pills and staying off my feet.
I go to bed early; I know I won't sleep.

I went to the doctor; he made an x-ray.
He said I was worse yesterday.
That made me feel better and I started to cry.
He said, "What's the matter?" I said I'm afraid I won't die.

The doctor has passed away and I'm still here.
I popped the pain pills; he drank the beer.
For me, beer he forbid.
He had arthritis a lot worse than I did.

I've quit popping pain pills; I'm feeling just fine.
If I live 'til December, I'll be 79.
Many of my friends had arthritis. They're in the ground.
I may live to be a hundred; I won't let it get me down.

FOURTH OF JULY PICNIC AT POSSUM HOLLOW

Pig pickin', chicken pickin', finger lickin'
Banjo pickin' blue grass;
Fiddle squeakin', cups leakin', babies sleepin', joints creakin'
Banjo pickin' blue grass.

Hot and sweatin', babies wettin', teenage pettin'
Banjo pickin' blue grass;
Hot dogs, cold dogs, cheese dogs, corn dogs
Banjo pickin' blue grass.

Watermelon, bellies swellin', people yellin', food smellin'
Banjo pickin' blue grass.

Hard liquor, beer and wine; that'll do it every time.
Banjo pickin' blue grass;
Hamburger half raw; Fight! Fight! Call the law.
Banjo pickin' blue grass.

Break it up! Break it up! Woman swallowed her snuff.
Banjo pickin'blue grass;
Bloody nose, torn clothes, whatta mess! Y'all are under arrest.
Banjo pickin' Blue grass.

Take'em to jail, book'em, out on bail; sick and pale; again
next year, oh, well;
Liquor, beer and wine; that'll do it every time.
Banjo pickin' blue grass.

RUN DOWN FARM

I worked myself to death on this run down farm;
Live in a house built like a barn.
People around here say I'm a fool,
Trying to make a living with a one-eyed mule.
Cow has gone dry; bucket's in the well. This place here
has gone to hell.

I went to the bank to get a loan.
The man said, "Do you own your home?"
I don't own nothing but a one-eyed mare.
He said I'd better go over to the welfare.

I see the preacher coming with his Bible in his hand.
He's going to tell me again about the Promised Land.
He's going to stay for dinner. He put his horse in the shed.
We ain't got nothing to eat but fat back meat and corn
bread.

We sat around on the front porch. He had his Bible in his hand.
He's going to tell me again about the Promised Land.
The preacher got sleepy, couldn't hold up his head.
While he was taking a nap, we ate all the fat back meat and corn bread.

SHOT GUN WEDDING

The wedding was on time as far as I could see.
Her daddy had a shot gun pointed right at me.
The preacher was very nervous and missed his place.
He read the entire book of Genesis; then sang "Amazing Grace".

Her daddy was aiming the shot gun; he had a mean eye.
The bride sniffed a time or two; the preacher began to cry.
The preacher stopped crying and started reading again.
He read the entire book of Exodus from beginning to end.

Her daddy waved the shot gun at me and pointed thumbs down.
He said I wouldn't be the first cradle robber he'd put in the ground.
The gun went off with a terrible roar; blasted a hole in the church floor. The bride got mad and with a sneer, shot down the chandelier.

The preacher grabbed his Bible and started to run.
She said, "Hold it, Preacher, your job ain't done."
Her daddy beat up on the preacher and landed in jail.
She flatly refused to go his bail.

There was some damage at the church; I don't know who paid the bill.
I hope I don't ever get into another mess like that as long as I live.

THE DAY BOBBY WENT TO SCHOOL

Bobby went to school today.
He didn't want to go but he went anyway.
When he got there the teacher was mad.
Some kid had given her a wormy apple and that was bad.

At the first bite what did she find?
A half a worm of the worst kind
The teacher said, "I don't think kids will ever learn."
Bobby raised his hand and said, "Teacher, I didn't know the apple had a worm."

The teacher said, "Bobby, you will sit in the corner,
Like little Jack Horner,
Without any curds and whey,

And write about Mary's lamb – a twenty-word essay".

This is what he wrote:
"Mary had a little lamb; its ears where white as snow.
And everywhere that Mary went the lamb didn't want to
go.
It followed her to school one day and learned the ABCs;
Then went on to college and got its Master's Degree from
UNC."

The teacher said, "Bobby, you are a poet and didn't know
it."
Bobby said, "I guess I have a lot to learn.
I am trying to figure out what happened to the other half of
that worm."

THE LIMO WAS A LEMON

I went uptown the other day,
Stopped at a car lot on my way.
A salesman came out and shook my hand
And said, "What can I do for you, my good man?"

I said, "I'm shopping for a car."
He said, "What kind do you have in mind?"
I said, "I'll take a Chevrolet any ole time."

He opened a little black book, then asked flat out,
"How much money are we talking about?"
I said, "About 50 grand."
He said, "Now we know where we stand.

This may sound a little strange.
We don't have a Chevrolet
In that price range.

I have a limo that I repossessed.
It has 100,000 on it, more or less.
I could let it go for 50 grand.
How does that sound to you, my good man?"

"What about the gas mileage –
Would you say eighteen?"
"Well, it's a gas guzzler
If you know what I mean."

When I got home the gas tank was dry as a bone.
I was stupid to put that much in it.
Like Barnum & Bailey said,
There's a sucker born every minute.

THE PREACHER

I see the preacher coming with a woman at his side.
He has been courting the Widow Johnson since her
husband died.
The preacher won't go anywhere without his Bible in his
hand.
He's gonna tell the Widow about the Promised Land.

He'll tell her about Noah's Ark and quote scripture from
the Book of Mark.

The Widow Johnson said, "Don't you ever get tired of talking?"
"Let's sit down; I'm tired of walking."
They sat down on a log under an old oak tree.
The preacher said, "When you decide to marry, will you marry me?"

She said, "I'll put you on my list."
"How far am I on that list? I'm getting old, you know."
She said, "Well, I can tell you this:
You are the low man on the totem pole."
The preacher walked the widow home and tried to steal a kiss.
She backed away and said, "Keep away, don't touch me.
I'm saving myself for my next husband to be."

I see the preacher coming with his Bible in his hand.
I don't think he feels like talking about the Promised Land.
He says he's weary and sick in his soul.
The Widow Johnson told him he's the low man on the totem pole.

TURN THAT DURN THING DOWN

Don't tell me about your mother-in-law; I've got one of my own.
She came to stay a day or two and stayed on and on.
She wakes everyone up at sunrise, turns the radio on and dances all around.
That's when the neighbors get on the phone and yell, "Turn that durn thing down."

Don't tell me about your mother-in-law; I've got one that takes the cake.
She's been saying she is going home since 1968.
We put her on the bus several years ago and told her to come again.
We headed for home and when we got there she was washing her hair and asked us where we'd been.

Don't tell me about your mother-in-law; I've got one that takes the prize.

She turns on the radio and wakes everyone up at sunrise.
She likes loud music; it makes her dance around.
That's when the neighbors get on the phone and yell, "Turn that durn thing down."

Don't tell me about your mother-in-law; I've got one that'll blow your mind.
This was a quiet neighborhood 'til she came to live with us in 1959.
All the neighbors are selling their houses and moving out of town.
The loud music has got to them cause she won't turn that durn thing down.

When she left this morning she said, "I shall return; blood
is thicker than water."
She said I had more sense than anybody – I married her
only daughter.

WHEN YOU PAY ME, I'LL PAY YOU

I had an appointment with the doctor at half past ten.
When I got there, the doctor wasn't in.
The nurse said, "He was supposed to be here at half past
eight;
I guess you'll just have to wait."

I waited and waited; the time dragged on.
The nurse came out and said, "I thought you'd gone home.
The doctor will be in at three.
He lost a golf ball up in a tree."

The doctor came in, looked in my eyes, nose and ears.
The nurse made an x-ray of my head.
The doctor looked at the x-ray and said, "Half of your brain
is dead."
I said, "Doc, I can't believe that."
The nurse said, "Oh my Lord, I forgot to take off his hat."

The doctor said, "I'm late for my date." The nurse said,
"Will you be on call?"
He said, "Don't call me; I'll be at the golf course looking
for my ball."
The nurse handed me a bill for one hundred and ten.
I said, "Goodbye, you won't see me again."

I lost seven hours from work – one hundred dollars and ten.
I went home; made out a bill to the doctor for one hundred dollars and ten;
"Please pay when due;
When you pay me, I'll pay you."

THE BABY'S STILL A-CRYING

I am looking through the keyhole from my bedroom door;
Papa's carrying the baby and he's walking the floor.
Mama's yelling at Papa and the baby is a-crying.
What Mama is yelling at Papa is no nursery rhyme.

Somebody called the police; they are knocking on the door.
Papa's not walking; he's laying on the floor.
Mama's yelling at the police; the baby's still a-crying.
What Mama's yelling at the police is no nursery rhyme.

Neighbors are looking through the windows at Papa on the floor.
The police have quit knocking; they are breaking down the door.
Mama's swinging a hammer; the baby's still a-crying.
What Mama's yelling at the neighbors is no nursery rhyme.

They put the cuffs on Mama and took her to the slammer.

She's charged with hitting Papa on the head with a
hammer.
She's in Cell No. 4 and the baby's still a-crying.
What Mama's yelling at the judge is no nursery rhyme.

Papa took the baby home; they are both a-crying,
Pacing back and forth across the floor and sighing;
Wondering what they're gonna do while Mama serves her
time.
What Papa's yelling at the baby is no nursery rhyme.

Romance and Love

BIG MOON

A little maid was strolling
　　　Among the roses so red,
A big moon was rolling
　　　In the sky overhead.
She stood there in the moonlight;
　　　The shadows grew dim,
And then she kissed a rosebud;
　　　The kiss meant for him.

So shine on, Big Moon –
　　　Go let your beams kiss his
face.
And tell him I'm waiting
　　　In the same old place.
Waiting in the garden
　　　Where the red roses bloom,

And I'm longing for his kisses
    In the light of the moon.

The big moon rolled onward
    Through the star lit sky,
And left the little maiden
    With tears in her eyes.
Moon beams kissed his face;
    It was her message of love,
And her prayers were answered
    By the Big Moon above.

I'M SO GLAD I FOUND HER IN A FIVE AND TEN CENT STORE

I went there to buy some sen-sen and a ten cent pocket
comb,
A five cent pack of chewing gum and a bottle of Hoyt's
cologne.
I fell in love with a girl at counter number four.
I'm so glad I found her in a five and ten cent store.

Sometimes I dream of going back to the five and ten cent
store,
Just to see who is working at counter number four
Somebody's sweetheart as mine did before.
I'm so glad I found her in a five and ten cent store.

When I woke up from dreaming, my memories are
bittersweet.
I look at her beside me and she is smiling in her sleep.

She's my one and only, I couldn't love her more.
I'm so glad I found her in a five and ten cent store.

I have boxes and boxes of sen-sen, ten cent pocket combs,
And at least one hundred bottles of Hoyt's cologne.
I think I got a bargain at counter number four.
I'm so glad I found her in a five and ten cent store.

The five and ten is gone now and so are the good ole days.
When they built the shopping malls, they changed our
shopping ways.
They don't have pretty girls at the counters anymore.
I'm so glad I found her in a five and ten cent store.

SHE'S MY BLUE RIDGE MOUNTAIN SWEETHEART

She's my Blue Ridge mountain sweetheart with her pretty
eyes of blue. Her lips are sweet as honey and her smile
comes shining through. We roamed the hills and valleys,
picked the flowers by the lane, Watched the sun rise over
the mountain after the early morning rain. She's my Blue
Ridge mountain sweetheart, I will love her 'til I die. We'll
always be together where the mountains meet the sky.

I'm going back to the Blue Ridge where I left my heart and
home; My rambling days are over, I never more will roam.
If this old bus keeps on rolling, I'll make it through all
right, Before the moon comes over the mountain, I'll be
back home tonight.
I'll pick a bouquet of mountain roses, one for each day I

stayed away; And every time I give them to her, this is
what I'll say,
"You are my Blue Ridge mountain sweetheart, our love
will never die. We'll always be together where the
mountains meet the sky."

It's a quiet time now on the Blue Ridge as twilight shadows
fall; The silence is broken only by a night bird's mating
call. She moves a little closer to me and gently takes my
hand, And then she softly whispers, "I love you, mountain
man." She's my Blue Ridge mountain sweetheart, our love
will never die. We'll always be together where the
mountains meet the sky.

I WISH I WERE EIGHTEEN AGAIN

When I was young I fell in love with every girl I met.
Even now there are one or two I can't forget.
Sometimes I think of all the good times that used to be.
I wonder if they ever think of me.

I wish I were eighteen again.
I wouldn't make the same mistakes I made back then.
Before I fell in love I'd count to ten.
I wish I were eighteen again.

Moonlight can make one do some crazy things,
Like dreaming of orange blossoms and wedding rings.
I had some crazy dreams back then.
I wish I were eighteen again.

I spent a lot of time in the old porch swing.
What was said there didn't mean anything.
She talked about the moon and stars above;
All I could think about was all the girls I'd loved.

I said, "Mama, I'm in love." She said, "It's puppy love.
You don't know what love is all about."
She was right – it was puppy love.
Now I'm glad that all the girls I loved chickened out.

Nature and Seasons

MOTHER NATURE

Autumn in Carolina, the leaves are turning brown.
There's a touch of winter in the air when the sun goes
down. Soon the cold winds will come and make us wish for
spring again.
The seasons must run their courses; that's the way it's
always been.

Mother Nature is full of surprises. She likes to put on
display. A beautiful sunrise, just to start another day.
An early morning rain – then after the clouds have cleared
away,
Across the sky comes a beautiful rainbow, as if to say,
"Isn't it a beautiful day?"

Mother Nature's world is perfect. It will stay that way 'til
the end.
Nothing is added; nothing is taken away. That's the way

it's always been.
Mother Nature has given us everything we need.
Every day she opens a door
For us to make this day better than the day before.

Mother Nature hovers and surrounds us with loving care.
Yet we mar and scar her world every day of every year.
Mother Nature is eternal. She'll be here when we are gone.
We must be responsible for our actions. We live here; this
is our home.

RAKING LEAVES

I cut the grass all summer;
Pushed that mower around.
Now there is no grass to cut;
The leaves have covered the ground.

I rake the leaves to the curb side
To be picked up now and then.
I looked outside this morning;
They were back in my yard again.

I pile 'em here and pile 'em there.
I got leaves in my pocket and leaves in my hair.
I raked sixteen tons today.
I'm hoping for a wind storm to blow these leaves away.

There's no doubt about it;
These leaves have got me goin'.
I'll be glad to see the grass again

So I can get back to mowin'.

The wind is a monster.
It makes my job real hard.
I can't understand why all the leaves in this block
Wind up in my front yard.

WHEN IT'S SPRING TIME ON THE BLUE RIDGE

When it's spring time on the Blue Ridge
The mountain roses are in bloom.
Wild flowers on every hill side
All nature is in tune.

When it's spring time on the Blue Ridge
Sweethearts stroll and pick flowers by the lane.
Watching the moon rise over the mountains
In a sudden burst of flame.

When it's spring time on the Blue Ridge
Twilight shadows fall around.
A gentle breeze is stirring
Making shadows on the ground.

When it's spring time on the Blue Ridge
Darkness pushes aside the shadows
And the quietness closes in. It's supper time on the Blue
Ridge.
It's time to pray again.

When it's spring time on the Blue Ridge
God has put everything in place.
We ask Him to bless us and the Blue Ridge
And we thank Him for His grace.

GOD PAINTS THE BLUE RIDGE

God painted the Blue Ridge Mountains with green, red and
gold, and took some colors from a rainbow and brought
them into the fold.
God then splashed some colors on the foothills just to catch
your eye, And painted a background of blue where the
mountains meet the sky.

God didn't forget the snow that will fall there very soon
Like diamonds on the colors woven on God's loom.
When God sees fit the leaves will leave the trees without a
sound
Once again showing their beauty making patterns on the
ground.

The trees have grown the harvest; now it's time for them to
rest. God smiles on them and said, "You have done your
best."
Now the trees stand like soldiers overcoming wind, snow
and rain. Waiting patiently for God to tell them to begin
making leaves again.

Year after year God paints the Blue Ridge where the
mountains meet the sky.
This is one of God's great miracles that He wants to show

you and I.
The seasons come and go; they work at His command.
By this we know that the world is in His hand.

MOUNTAIN ROSES

Pick a bouquet of mountain roses,
    Kiss them with the morning dew.
Tie them together with a sunbeam,
    Wrap them up in heaven's blue.

Take a rainbow from the heavens,
    Wrap around them so nice and neat.
Sprinkle on them a little star dust
    Just to keep them fresh and sweet.

You'll find them growing on some lonely hill,
    Growing, oh so wild and free.
Bring them down and place them on my grave,
    They'll be happy there with me.

Pick a bouquet of mountain roses,
    Put them on my grave for me.
You'll find them in North Carolina, Virginia and
Tennessee.
    Be sure to pick them in the spring time,
While they are in their beauty rare.
    Pick them all, don't leave one to bloom alone,
It will be too lonely there.

Soon they'll fade and die and be blown away
    By the winds from the mountains high;
But they'll grow and bloom again some day
    For me up in the sky.

SUMMER TIME IN MY BACK YARD

A redheaded woodpecker pecking on a tree,
Pecking out a tune to the humming of the bees.
A blue jay high up in a tree,
Quarreling with my tom cat hidden in the leaves.

Squirrels digging up nuts hidden in the ground,
Bumblebees buzzing round and around.
Butterflies sitting on a marigold,
Ants busy making a hole.

Blackbirds and sparrows searching the ground;
Twilight shadows falling around.
Lightning bugs wink here and there;
The scent of honeysuckle is in the air.

The woodpecker is silent now; the blue jay is in its nest.
My tom cat comes out of hiding and lays down at my feet
to rest.
All is quiet now in my back yard and the quietness is hard
to define.
Some people like the winter but I like the summer time.

Blues

A BORN LOSER

I'll never get used to that jail house smell
No matter how well I clean my cell.
It always smells like someone else,
Like a bunch of buffalo pelts.

My cell is four by four feet square.
I counted the bars; they are still there.
It ain't big enough for anybody else.
If I'm not careful, I'll step on myself.

I see the warden coming; he's gonna shoot me a line.
He's gonna tell me I've done my time.
He thinks I don't remember when they brought me in.
It's been a long time ago, but I remember when.

I'll get out when I'm 92.
My girlfriend said she'd wait, but they never do.
She said, "Cross my heart and hope to die."
I knew right then she was telling a lie.
She got married to my best friend
The same day he got out and I got in.

HEARTACHES AND TEARDROPS

Heartaches and teardrops and too many regrets;
Bittersweet memories I just can't forget.
Lonely and crying all through the night;

Tears on my pillow when the sun gives its light.

I dread for the night but I know it must come.
Shadows fall around me and the birds hush their song.
Loneliness surrounds me and withers my soul.
No one here to love me and my heart has grown cold.

I see things around me that bring me regret;
Things that remind me I'd like to forget.
No one to talk to, no one to care;
A heart full of heartaches and my eyes full of tears.

I lie in bed, sleep just won't come.
I look at the stars and wish I were one;
Up in the heavens where it's peaceful and quiet;
Where there's no heartaches, no teardrops at night.

I'LL THROW AWAY THE RING

I called and asked her if she had set the date
For our wedding day.
As I waited, she hesitated
As if she didn't know just what to say.

Then I knew that something had happened,
And the phone trembled in my hand.
Then I heard her softly saying
She had married another man.

I still have the ring that she'll never wear,
And I still have the house that we'll never share.

The rooms are empty and the walls are bare.
It's a house of desolation and despair.

Now time has healed my broken heart
And eased my wounded pride.
What good is a little band of gold,
If there is no blushing bride?

I hope she finds true happiness
And the best of everything.
There'll never be anyone else for me,
So I'll just throw away the ring.

SAW MILL MAN

Working at the saw mill all day long,
Listening to the saw blades sing their song
I sing mine along with them
From 6 in the morning 'til 6 p.m.

I work for a dollar; get paid every day
And take all the work that comes my way.
Got to make a living the best I can;
I'm a hard working saw mill man.

Let the saw dust fly; keep those logs coming through.
Got to make a dollar; baby needs a new pair of shoes.
Everybody wants lumber – mill is running overtime.
I hope I can make some extra money so I can pay my rent
on time.

If I'm lucky I get some overtime; work a double shift
And make an extra dollar to get my baby a quart of milk.
The double shift is over; no more logs on the ground.
They've quit building houses 'til the interest rate comes
down.

I'll go home to my wife and baby and do the best I can.
And when they start the mill again
Maybe they'll need a saw mill man.

SCUM LIKE YOU WILL NEVER TAKE MY TOWN

The two men stood face to face in the street.
Each had hoped they would never meet.
The morning sun flashed on their guns;
Two shots rang out as one.
They lay dead; their guns in their hands.
Each thought they were faster than the other man.

The sheriff came out and looked them over.
"Too bad," he said, "I liked Frank and Grover."
They buried them on Boothill with the rest
Who thought they were the best.

The two men stood face to face in the street.
Each had hoped they would never meet.
Their guns spit flame in the evening sun;
Two shots rang out as one.
They lay dead with their guns in their hands.
Each thought he was faster than the other man.

The sheriff came out; turned them over with his toe.
"Too bad," he said, "I liked Bill and Joe."
They buried them on Boothill with the rest
Who thought they were the best.

The town was quiet for the rest of the night.
The card game was in high gear.
The whiskey was flowing again and so was the beer.
Across the street in the Greasy Spoon,
The old piano was banging out a tune.

The sheriff washed his face; strapped on his gun.
He muttered to himself, "This is the worst job under the
sun."
He stepped out in the morning sun.
A man said, "Sheriff, drop your gun,
Me and my men are taking this town."

A shot rang out from the Blacksmith Shop.
The gunman went down without firing a shot.
The sheriff heard four horses heading out of town.
He walked over to the man on the ground
And said, "Scum like you will never take my town."

THE END OF THE AMERICAN DREAM

I wanted to be counted in the Middle Class
And live like the people next door.
They drive a big, black Cadillac.
I drive a beat-up Ford.

I work sixteen hours every day
While the sweat runs down my face.
It's dog-eat-dog in a crazy world.
I'm caught up in the old rat race.

I wanted a house in the country
And lots of real estate;
A chain link fence all around it,
With my name on the big front gate.

I wanted a big, black Cadillac;
And a great big house on a hill;
A big, green lawn; a swimming pool;
And a dozen steaks on the grill.

I've never lived high on the hog.
I'm tired of these pork and beans.
My life is just another nightmare.
It's the End of the American Dream.

THE RETIREMENT BLUES

I've got the retirement blues and I'm feeling mighty low,
Waiting for the postman and he's walking mighty slow.
It's the third of the month and today I collect
My Social Security retirement check.

I got up this morning, ate my breakfast with the blues,
Didn't feel like bending over to tie my shoes.
Just a-sitting and a-rocking in my old rocking chair.
If I don't lose these retirement blues,

I'm gonna rock away from here.

I'll never make it to Heaven on that Judgment Day,
Just a-sitting and a-rocking watching the TV play.
Just a-sitting and a-rocking in my old rocking chair.
If I don't lose these retirement blues,
I'm gonna rock away from here.

I've got arthritis in these bones of mine,
Just a-sitting and a-rocking waiting for the summertime.
Just a-sitting and a-rocking in my old rocking chair.
If I don't lose these retirement blues,
I'm gonna rock away from here.

It's getting late in the evening and I still have the blues,
Just a-sitting and a-rocking watching the six o'clock news.
Just a-sitting and a-rocking in my old rocking chair.
If I don't lose these retirement blues,
I'm gonna rock away from here.

THE WEEPING WILLOW WEEPS FOR SOMEBODY (BUT NOBODY WEEPS FOR ME)

The judge he said, "I'll give you life."
It cut my heart just like a knife.
I sit in jail; don't get no mail.
Nobody comes to go my bail.
I'm a three time losing man.
The weeping willow weeps for somebody,
But nobody weeps for me.

They bring my food on a plate of tin,
And remind me of what I might have been.
They know I'm a loner, they know I'm a goner.
That's why I ran.
Now they know I'm a three time losing man.
The weeping willow weeps for somebody,
But nobody weeps for me.

When they lay me down to my sweet rest,
There'll be no flowers on my breast;
Just a coffin of pine, nobody crying.
I'm a three time losing man.
The weeping willow weeps for somebody,
But nobody weeps for me.

I know I'll die here; it will be slow.
I can see sweet chariots swinging low,
To take me away to that bright land.
This time I won't be a three time losing man.
The weeping willow weeps for somebody,
But nobody weeps for me.

WORKING IN THE COTTON MILL
ALL DAY LONG (Thomas C. Green, seated left playing guitar)

Working in the cotton mill all day long,
Listening to the spindles sing their song.
I sing mine along with them,
From six in the morning 'til six p.m.

I was called a lint head and poor white trash,
In the Twenties when the market crashed.
Rich men cried when they heard the news.
I didn't worry – had nothing to lose.

Blue shabby shirt, a pair of blue jeans;
Cornbread and taters, pinto beans;
Black-eyed peas, collard greens;
Fat back meat – no streak o'lean.

Working in the cotton mill all day long,
Listening to the spindles sing their song.
Never see the sun rise, watching the clock;
Waiting for pay day to spend what I got.

CHORUS

Gotta keep 'em humming, boss is around.
Day's nearly done and the sun's gone down.
Working in the cotton mill all day long,
It's six p.m. and I'm gonna go home.
Gonna eat my cornbread and black-eyed peas.
Then I'm gonna rest and take my ease.
"Fore I go to sleep I'm gonna kneel and pray;
Ask the good Lord for one more day.
Working in the cotton mill all day long,
Listening to the spindles sing their song.
I sing mine along with them,
From six in the morning 'til six p.m.

HURTING INSIDE

Hurting inside and hiding my tears,
Loving her always, but she didn't care.
While she was flirting with some other guy,
I was hiding my tears and hurting inside.

I should have known she couldn't be true,
She was always looking for somebody new,
I knew she was trouble but I couldn't let go.
I tried to forget her but my heart said no.

I was hurting inside and hoping she'd change;
She kept on flirting and playing the game.
Now it's all over and I don't care,
I'm not hurting inside and I've dried up my tears.

I've dried up my tears and hold up my head,
And face the world squarely without any dread.
The past is forgotten; the future is clear.
I've quit hurting inside and dried up my tears.

It's a great feeling to be free again.
I can start all over – this time I'll win.
My heart is lighter, my conscience is clear.
I've quit hurting inside and dried up my tears.

COUNTING MY LIFE AWAY

The lights are still on in the jury room.
The clock in the tower strikes three.
No one is talking while the guards are walking,
And there is no sleep for me.

The jury's been out for three days and three nights
Deciding what my fate shall be.
They can send me to the pen for the rest of my life,
Or it could be the chair for me.

I've counted the roaches that race back and forth.
I've counted the mice in the trash.
I've counted the flies that buzz overhead,
And I've counted the guards that pass.

I want to be free just once more to see
The stars through my own window pane.
But after this night, they'll be out of sight,
And I'll never see them again.

I've counted the bars around me
A thousand times or more.
I've counted the chains that bind me,
And I've counted the cracks in the floor.

I've counted the days, months, and years.
There is no end in sight.
The only thing that means anything
Is counting the stars at night.

Faith

BACK IN THE FOLD AGAIN

I was lonely and forsaken, couldn't face another day.
Feeling so despondent, I knelt and began to pray.
I asked the Lord to forgive me of all my sin.
He put his arms around me—I'm back in the fold again.

Like a lost sheep on a mountain, a prodigal without a home
Like Peter I denied the Lord Jesus, the best friend I'd ever
known.
Time and time again I denied him and when I needed a
friend
He put his arms around me—I'm back in the fold again.

I shouted "Hallelujah!" I'm not bound by sin.
He broke the chains that bound me and set me free again.
I felt his hand upon me; my heart nearly burst within
When he put his arms around me—I'm back in the fold
again.

I heard the angels singing, "The Devil cannot win."
I heard the Lord Jesus proclaiming, "He's back in the fold
again."
Now I'm not forsaken; now I have a friend
Protected by the power of Jesus—back in the fold again.

DUST THOU ART

After Adam ate the apple he knew that he had sinned
And sealed the fate of mankind from the beginning of time
to the end.
He didn't know that God was coming in the cool of the

day.

Adam and Eve were afraid and hid themselves away.
God said, "Adam, you have disobeyed my command.
For the rest of your life, you will till the land.
Starting right now
You will earn your living by the sweat of your brow.

You will live 930 years.
At your death, you'll regret what you have done 'til your
last breath. You will work and sweat, know sorrow, grief,
pain, and death.
All these lessons you will learn
For dust thou art and dust thou shall return."

We are walking in Adam and Eve's footprints.
We are going through what they went through.
There is still one lesson to be learned:
That we came from dust and back to dust we will return.

GOD KNOWS WHAT IS BEST FOR ME

I won't worry about tomorrow;
What is to be will be.
I won't worry about tomorrow;
God knows what is best for me.

I won't worry about tomorrow;
Tomorrow I may never see.
I won't worry about tomorrow;
God knows what is best for me.

I won't worry about tomorrow;
God will supply all my needs.
I won't worry about tomorrow;
God knows what is best for me.

I won't worry about tomorrow;
The future is not for me to see.
I won't worry about tomorrow;
God knows what is best for me.

I won't worry about tomorrow;
I know where I'll spend eternity.
I won't worry about tomorrow;
God knows what is best for me.

GOD WAS WITH US

I'd like to go back to the old days when times were slower.
We didn't have much money but the prices were lower.
We took care of each other, shared what we had.
I couldn't tell the difference between the good times and
the bad.

It was hard to make ends meet; didn't have money to spare.
The Government didn't hand out free food; we had no
welfare.
Now there are food stamps which make life a little better.
The only stamp we knew about was the stamp we put on a
letter.

It was hard times from nineteen hundred to nineteen fifty-
five.
We lived through two world wars, the great depression and
we survived.
We came through with blood, sweat and tears.
Without God's grace and mercy, we could not make it
through those years.

When you hear the words, "home of the brave and land of
the free,"
Remember that's for you and me.
And when you hear the words, "rockets bursting in air,"
Remember God was there.
Now when we salute Old Glory, stand straight and tall.
Don't forget to give God the glory; He was with us through
it all.

JESUS TOOK AWAY MY HEARTACHE

Jesus took away my heartache and gave me peace of mind.
He broke the chains that bound and tied the tie that binds.
He took away my heartache and cleansed my soul of sin
When I opened my heart and let him in.

Now He's in my heart to stay; I talk to him night and day.
I can't live without Him; I need Him all the time.
He shared my grief and sorrow and knew why I was crying.
He took away my heartache and gave me peace of mind.
He took away temptation and gave the strength to say,
"Get behind me, Satan, I have more power than you today."
He knew how weak I was and how hard I was trying.

He took away my heartache and gave me peace of mind.

Jesus took away my heartache and gave me peace of mind.
Now He's put it back together, one piece at a time –
Faith, hope and love for all mankind.
Jesus took away my heartache and gave me peace of mind.

NO RED LIGHTS IN HEAVEN

No red lights in Heaven
No one way streets to get on
No left turn lanes to confuse us
One straight street will lead home

No drinking and driving in Heaven
No bodies to pull from a wreck
No sound of a siren in the distance
To make us wonder if we will be next

No cheating, no greed in Heaven
No inflation, no fighting for oil
The air will be pure in Heaven
No pollution will fall on the soil

No war and killing in Heaven
No hungry children in the world
No different races in Heaven
Only one flag to unfurl

Christ will reign over the nations
His reign never will fall

God's will be done by his only son
He'll reign with truth and justice for all

THE BEST PART OF THE DAY

When the song birds hush their singing,
And the evening shadows fall;
The silence is broken now and then,
By the night bird's mating call.

When the dew drops on the willows,
And there's the scent of fresh cut hay;
And God's creatures are resting;
This is the best part of the day.

The twilight wraps around me
Like a blanket soft and warm;
While God walks on the clouds of heaven,
Keeping me safe from all harm.

The angel choir is singing
As the moon beams bathe my face.
I bow my head in reverence
And thank God for his mercy and his grace.

WHEN THE DAY IS DONE

Too many heartaches and too many regrets;
Bittersweet memories I don't want to forget;
Too many long hours to make ends meet;
Too many long nights without any sleep.

Too many worries and too many cares;
It's not over yet; I still have the tears.
I never thought life would be easy or that I had it made.
I always faced reality and called a spade a spade.

Life is a testing ground, testing me to the fullest.
It's up to me to stand the test and bite the bullet.
No one else can do it for me. My mother said it would be
this way.
I call on God to renew my spirit and give me strength for
today.

When I get tired and weary, I have to rest.
The Devil never sleeps; he's doing what he does best.
He uses every trick to lead me astray.
But God will not let him have his way.

One day at a time is all that I can handle;
Tomorrow is yet to come.
I'll challenge all the Devil has to offer,
And I'll be the winner when the day is done.

REMEMBER WHEN YOU PRAY

Keep your heart light and gay;
    Don't ever run away
From the things that worry you
    And make you frown.
Just remember when you pray,
    Ask the good Lord every day

To help you with the things
    That get you down.

Sometimes we have a notion
    Everything is out of proportion.
It only makes us fume, fret and frown.
    Remember when you pray
Ask the good Lord every day
    To help you with the things
That get you down.

There's a thousand things
    That put you in a strain,
And runs your pressure up
    A hundred or two.
But have you ever stopped to think
    That you may be
The thing that makes all these
    Worries happen to you?
Remember when you pray,
    Ask the good Lord every day
To help you with the things
    That get you down.
You don't have to preach a sermon,
    Nor sing the songs of Zion,
Nor go around a moaning,
    Your eyes all red from crying.
Just give the Lord a chance;
    He'll tell you what to do.
He'll never let you down.
    He'll always see you through.

Remember when you pray,
    Ask the good Lord every day
To help you with the things
    That get you down.

FLOWERS FOR MY SAVIOUR

When my spirit leaves this body
And its earthly scars,
God will give me a new body,
Bright and shining as the stars.

When my journey ends,
I'll rest for a thousand years;
And God will empty the bottle
That He filled with my tears.

And when they fall from Heaven,
Scattered from sea to shining sea,
I pray they'll fall on those I love,
And give them peace and tranquility.

I hope God will fill the bottle with flowers,
That I planted along the way;
And that He will keep them 'til Resurrection Day,
When He calls me from the grave – there'll be flowers for
my Saviour.

Thomas C. Green

PLACE YOUR HAND IN MINE

I went down to the river,
To find some peace and quiet.
I found a beautiful place;
I stayed throughout the night.

The whisper of the river
Was the only sound.
It was like I pictured heaven
And I knelt there on the ground.

Jesus laid his hand upon me.
I felt a joy within
When he said, "I've come to help you,
If you'll confess all your sins.
Don't wait 'til tomorrow, now is the time.
This is the day of salvation.
Place your hand in mine."

Place your hand in mine; I'll go with you all the way,
Throughout the valley of the shadow if you'll trust and
obey. Place your hand in mine and believe on my name.
Lord, I'm not worthy; I hung my head in shame.
I placed my hand in his where the nails had been
And believed on his name; He forgave all my sins.

THE WORLD NEEDS FIXING

The world needs fixing; it has a broken heart.
Only God can fix it. He has the spare parts.

The world could well be at the brink of death.
Only God can fix it, before it breathes its last breath.

The world struggles in agony, moans, and groans
While the sun rises and sets and time moves on.
The Devil waits with patience, hoping the world will fall
apart and die.
He wants God defeated and to see the angels cry.

Thank God the moon still lights the world at night.
The stars in all their glory shoot across the sky.
The seasons come and go; with them come the sunshine,
rain and snow.
God says, "The world is mine. I created it. I will fix it in
due time."

The Devil says the fires are lit
In the bottomless pit.
The Devil laughs with glee.
"The doors are open and I am ready
To take the world to Hell with me."

Community, Country
and Patriotism

BEWARE
There's a con man on every corner with his slick and slimy
ways.
He's waiting to stick it to you and he knows a hundred
ways.
He's doing what he does best; rip you off.
He'll sell you a band aid and tell you it will cure your
hacking cough.

There's a pusher on every corner waiting to fix you up.
He wants you to sit at the Devil's table and drink from the
Devil's cup.
He doesn't want your money, your silver, nor your gold.
His aim is to destroy your body as well as your soul.

There's a gunman on every corner waiting to shoot you
down.
You are not his enemy; he just don't like seeing you
around.
He's a born killer, never learned to read.
He kills just for the fun of it; he likes to see you bleed.

There's a big mouth, know-it-all in every discussion; he
knows it all from A to Z.
He got his information from reading tabloids and watching
T.V.
His brain is mostly negative; the positive part is dead.

His mouth is always working: What he needs is a smaller hole in his head.

BROTHER, CAN YOU SPARE A DIME?

I walk the streets at midnight looking for a place to sleep.
The snow is coming down heavy, turning to sleet.
I'll wash dishes for my breakfast.
I can't help being homeless; it's no fault of mine.
I'll be on the streets tomorrow. Brother, can you spare a dime?

I'm cold, hungry and homeless; tears run down my face.
The way I have to live is not fit for the human race.
People look at me and put me down as being trash.
I can't help being homeless; it's no fault of mine.
I'll be on the streets tomorrow. Brother, can you spare a dime?

We burn our dreams in an oil drum and watch them go up in smoke. And don't blame each other for being homeless; we're all in the same boat.
Our government has forsaken us; they worship the golden calf.
Someday the Lord will separate the wheat from the chaff.
I can't help being homeless; it's no fault of mine.
I'll be on the streets tomorrow. Brother, can you spare a dime?
We sit around the oil drum; the fire is burning low.
I see my world turned upside down in its feeble glow.
I'm cold, hungry and homeless; tears run down my face.

I'm proud of who I am, but I'm disgusted with the human race.
I can't help being homeless; it's no fault of mine.
I'll be on the streets tomorrow. Brother, can you spare a dime?

I JUST HAVE TO HAVE THAT GASOLINE

When the time comes and I can't buy any more,
I'll drain the gas from my old lawn mower.
No doubt about it, I can't do without it.
I just have to have that gasoline.

I'll drive my car 'til the tank runs dry
And fight the Arabs 'til I die.
No doubt about it, I can't do without it.
I just have to have that gasoline.

I'll walk old Hussein across the sand,
Make him carry my gasoline can.
No doubt about it, I can't do without it.
I just have to have that gasoline.

If there is one thing I live for,
It's to have a tank full of gas in my car.
No doubt about it, I can't do without it.
I just have to have that gasoline.

JOHN DOE

With the point of a needle, he opened a vein
And pushed a shot of cocaine into his brain.
His eyes glazed over; his face turned white.
He was out like a light for the rest of the night.

His body was found in a dumpster, his head caved in.
They don't have a clue as to who threw him in.
The police asked a lot of people, "Do you know this man?"
They said, "No."
His body is at the morgue with a tag on his toe – another
John Doe.

They took him to the cemetery in a coffin of pine.
There were no mourners, nobody crying.
Then the preacher said a short prayer and asked again,
"Does anybody know this man?" All answered, "No."
May God have mercy on John Doe.

The pusher keeps them dangling like a monkey on a string
Until he sells his soul for a shot of cocaine.
The Devil and his demons dance around his tomb,
Gloating over the infected still in the womb.

POLLUTION
THEY HAD TO LEAVE THE TOWN

I looked at the river with tears in my eyes,
And watched the pollution float down with the tide.
I felt sorry for the river. It's sick, I said to myself,

Choking and dying, waiting for death.

The river's purity and beauty has been destroyed by man.
God is watching the pollution and the raping of the land.
Man has scarred the face of nature; these acts I will record.
You'll be held responsible when you come face to face
with the Lord.

The pollution in the river goes along with the flow until it
hits the dam.
Now the people have no drinking water; they will have to
leave the town.

Dear God, make a river. Let it be pure all the way to the
sea.
Let it tell the story of what God can do for you and me.
Mankind is not satisfied with what God has made.
They want to destroy and make it the way they want it
made.

THE BOTTOM OF THE SPOON

A shot of cocaine in the bottom of a spoon,
Pumped in his veins sent him to the moon.
He was out two days; he never knew where he'd been.
The doctor said he'd never use his brain again.

He gave up his future for a trip to the moon
And a shot of cocaine from the bottom of a spoon.
He spends his days staring into space;
All he can see is the devil's face.

His nights are filled with dreams like a merry-go-round that never
Comes around;
A Ferris wheel that goes up but never comes down.
The devil dances and says, "Come on, be happy, I'll call the tune
With a shot of cocaine from the bottom of a spoon."

The devil threw a party; it lasted all night.
He passed the spoon around for another shoot before daylight.
That's the last shot they'll ever take;
They were all dead before daybreak.

They danced while the devil called the tune
And died from an overdose from the bottom of the spoon.

THE BROTHERHOOD OF MAN

I am proud to be a Master Mason
And wear the Masonic ring.
When I put on the white apron,
I feel I can overcome anything.

I sign the book of members
And step into the Temple.
The atmosphere is cordial,
And everything is simple.

I feel safe and secure here.

I see no hate, no malice, no envy, no greed.
I am at peace with God and man.
I have no fear.

Here I took the obligation to be a Mason every day,
To control my passion and help a Brother along the way.
I'll stand by a Brother when he needs me, even go the extra mile;
Forgive a Brother seventy times seven with a handshake and a smile.

Long after I've left the Temple,
I feel the touch of a Brother's hand.
In my heart I'm satisfied that I've been
In the presence of God and the Brotherhood of Man.

Gate City Lodge 694
Scottish Rite 32°

THROUGH THE EYES OF A COP
THE NIGHT SHIFT

I have seen a blind man on a filthy bed.
I have seen a little child crying for bread.
I have seen the old and the gray.
I have seen the homeless on the highway.

I have seen the sick and the lame on hospital beds.
I have seen the ambulances bring in the dead.
I have seen a wino with a bottle of wine.
Through a broken window I heard a woman crying.

I have seen a battered woman, a victim of rape.
I have seen a little child with blood on his face.
I have seen a drug addict sniffing cocaine.
I have seen the spasms when it cooked his brain.

I have seen street fights and teenage gangs.
They fought like dogs with snarling fangs.
I have seen the flame of blazing guns and bloody knives.
I have seen broken bones and blood shot eyes.

I have seen young blood spilled in vain,
Washed away by summer rain.
The streets are quiet, it's nearly dawn.
My shift is over; I'll check out for home.

WE ARE TAKING BACK OUR STREETS AND SIDEWALKS

Turn on your porch light, unlock your door.
We are fed up with crime and we won't take anymore.
We are taking back our streets and sidewalks where we
used to walk.
It's time for action; there has been too much talk.

If you are a criminal, by now you should know,
We are taking back our streets and sidewalks. You'll have
to go.
We are fed up and mean what we say,
Don't wait 'til tomorrow. We want you off the streets
today.

We are taking back our streets and sidewalks.
We've been held hostage behind locked windows and

doors.
We are fed up with crime and criminals. We won't take it
anymore.

You have caused us pain and suffering, disrupted our peace
of mind.
Pack up your guns, pills and cocaine and move on down the
line.
We are taking back our streets and sidewalks. We won't
back down.
What we want to see is the dust from your screeching tires
when you leave this town.

WHAT CAN I DO WITH THIS NEW DAY OF MINE?

Yesterday is gone; it's after midnight.
I see the dawn; a new day is in sight.
What can I do with this new day of mine?
I won't waste it away; I don't have that much time.

I'll feed the hungry; give the orphans a home.
I'll keep in touch with the old folks that live all alone.
I'll visit the rest homes and brush their silvery hair;
Give them a hug and tell them that I care.

I'll talk to a wino. He may ask me for wine.
I'll buy him a meal and do without mine.
I'll talk to a drug addict, hooked on cocaine.
I'll pray with him in Jesus' name.

I'll go to the funeral home where reality seems unreal;

I'll tell all the grieving families I know just how they feel.
I'll go to the cemetery and stand by their side;
I'll be there to comfort them when they say their last
goodbye.

I'll give hope to the prisoners behind steel doors.
I'll pay tribute to the veterans that fought in the wars.
I won't get any medals for my busy day;
I'll sleep better knowing I didn't waste it away.

WHO WON THE WAR?

No flowers in the desert
No birds to sing their songs
No trees to cast a shadow
Only silence greets the dawn.

When the war is over
And the guns are stilled,
Then we'll count the bodies
Of those that were killed.

When the count is finished
And the casualties accounted for,
The question is still unanswered.
Who won the war?

Why send our sons and daughters
To fight and die on foreign soil
To satisfy the warmongers

And for a barrel of Saudi oil?

We'll pay 40 dollars for
Every barrel we use.
We are the suckers,
Win or lose.

YOU'VE COME A LONG WAY, BABY

You can be the top gun or a part-time sales clerk.
You can stay at home and have babies if you want.
You don't have to stay married to a jerk.

You can be the one to give the orders.
You can be the one that scrubs the floor.
You can be a part-time secretary.
You can be the Chairman of the Board.

You've come a long way, baby! Reach up and touch a star.
You can be anything you want to be from where you are.
Baby, you've come a long way; don't look back.
What has happened in the past won't happen anymore;
You've got your foot in the door.

You don't have to take harassment nor be pinched on the butt.
You can take a guy to court for calling you a slut.
If you're married to an alcoholic and he's addicted to a drug,
You don't have to put up with that; you can smash him like a bug.

You can own a Cadillac or hire a limousine.
You can drive a Ford Escort and pump your own gasoline.
You can be a governor, Supreme Court judge, lawyer, doctor
And maybe, just maybe, some day,
You can be President of the U.S.A.

You've come a long way, baby! Reach up and touch a star.
You can be anything you want to be from where you are.
Baby, you've come a long way; don't look back.
What has happened in the past won't happen anymore;
You've got your foot in the door.

Woman: God's crown jewel of His creations, mother of all living. Genesis 3:20

PLEASE DON'T BURN OUR FLAG TODAY

You have the right to speak,
Be careful of what you say.
Don't run down our country.
Please don't burn our flag today.

Think of the blood that was shed.
Think of the wounded and the dead.
Think of the cruel hands that would snatch it away.
Please don't burn our flag today.

Think of the veterans that cry in the night.
In their dreams they're back in the fight.
Think of the widows and orphans, their memories hidden away.
Please don't burn our flag today.

Think of the cold winter wind and stifling heat.
Think of the burning lungs and the frozen feet.
Think of the dead bodies and the stink and decay.
Please don't burn our flag today.

Think of the POW's kept in a cage,
Living on bread and water while their enemies cursed and raved.
They thought of home and loved ones, waited and prayed.
Please don't burn our flag today.

SOCIAL SECURITY?

Her hair had turned to silver. She could hardly move around
In the two room shack by the railroad track, the loneliest part of town.
She was listening to the radio and she almost had a stroke,
When the newsman came on to say that Social Security was broke.

She went to bed that night, but couldn't go to sleep.
She worried about how to pay the rent and buy food to eat.
They found her the next morning. She had gone to a better

place.
Without Social Security, the future she could not face.

Cruel words and uncertainties that old folks have to bear;
Shoulders bent with aches and pains and burdened down
with care.
Put your arms around them and smooth their silver hair.
Kiss their wrinkled cheek and tell them that you care.

The report came on the news tonight:
Social Security is breathing its last breath.
Before the sun comes up tomorrow,
Someone's poor old mother will worry herself to death.

Family

I AIN'T GONNA GO TO A NURSING HOME

Don't push me, just leave me alone.
I ain't gonna go to a nursing home.
I make my breakfast, make my bed,
Take my bath and wash my head.
I wash the dishes, scrub the pans,
Chew my tobacco, spit in a can.

Don't push me, just leave me alone.
I ain't gonna go to a nursing home.
I feed my Tom cat, brush his fur.
He lays in my lap and purrs and purrs.
They say, "Why don't you go to the mall?"

When you are 80 years old, you've seen it all.

Don't push me, just leave me alone.
I ain't gonna go to a nursing home.
I don't go to the movies; I've got nothing to lose.
I can see "Dick Tracey" on the 6 o'clock news.
Bank robberies, car chases, shoot out at the old corral;
Donald Trump's got a new gal.

Don't push me, just leave me alone.
I ain't gonna go to a nursing home.
I want to die in my own bed with my own pillow under my head.
My family won't push me; they'll leave me alone.
Thank God, I won't have to die in a nursing home.

I COULDN'T HANG MY ONLY SON

I hear the hammers pounding, driving in the nails.
They are building a scaffold beside this dirty jail.
The pounding and the sawing goes on and on.
They say they are going to hang me at the break of dawn.

I see the sheriff making the hangman's knot to fit behind my ear.
I ate my last meal; two soda crackers and a mug of warm beer.
I hear music coming from the saloon across the way.
They'll be playing "Swing Low Sweet Chariot" at the break of day.

I heard someone fumbling with the lock;
The sheriff came in at five o'clock.
Then he took his guns from a peg,
And tied each holster to his leg.
He spun the cylinder and checked the load.
He said, "Son, it's time to hit the road."

"Where are we going?" I asked in surprise.
"I thought you were going to hang me at sunrise."
The sheriff put the light out, put his badge on the desk, as
we went out the door.
He said, "I'm not the sheriff of this town anymore."
The horses were waiting at the rail.
The town was quiet when we hit the trail.
I said, "Do you realize what you've done?"
He said, "I couldn't hang my only son."

CINDY

I know a little girl named "Cindy",
    With her baby smile she can win ye.
She's never still, always on the go;
    If she gets attention, she puts on a show.
Better watch out –
    She can just about
Steal your heart away.

She's a little coy, she's a little shy,
    And there's a little mischief in her eye.
She can be good and she can be bad,
    She stomps her foot when she gets mad.

Better watch out –
    She can just about
Steal your heart away.

If you take her shopping, she's always stopping,
    She wants these and those;
She doesn't want toys, she doesn't want dolls;
    She just wants pretty clothes.
Better watch out –
    She can just about
Steal your heart away.

When she's dressed up in her Sunday best,
    She's like a blue bird in its nest.
Eyes all a-shining, hair in a curl;
    Now she's ready to be somebody's girl.
So you better watch out –
    She can just about
Steal your heart away.

Memories and Home

I'M GOING BACK TO GEORGIA

I'm going back to Georgia to the place where I was born
In the middle of December on a cold and frosty morn.
I made it through that winter at my Mama's side
On the back of a one-eyed mule – that's where I learned to ride.

I rode that mule everywhere. His name was Smoky Joe.

I rode him to town. We went to a picture show.
We sat in the balcony. He brayed a time or two.
They came and threw us out before the show was through.

I wanted to be a farmer. My Papa showed me how.
In less than 15 minutes I was walking behind a plow.
The next morning we were plowing at the break of dawn.
We plowed all day 'til supper time. Then we headed home.

When I got home I was so weary I was nearly dead.
We put the mules in the stable and hung the harness in the
shed.
The cow needed milking; the hogs had busted out;
The dogs had scared the chickens. They were running all
about.

Mama was on the back porch with a lantern in her hand.
She said times would be better when we got to the
Promised Land.
Papa said the blessing. I bowed my weary head.
He asked God to bless America and the black-eyed peas
and corn bread.

THERE'S NO PLACE LIKE HOME

I want to settle down in a one-horse town where everyone
knows my name
Shake hands and say, "Howdy," and everyone does the
same.
I want to hear the church bells; I'm tired of rock and roll
I want to hear the preaching and the Gospel songs, while
the Spirit fills my soul.

I want to settle down in a one-horse town where everyone
knows my name.
I want to walk to the cow pasture, sit around and watch a
baseball game;
Pitch horseshoes on the playground, play checkers in the
shade,
Smell the magnolias and feel like I've got it made.

I want to settle down in a one-horse town where everyone
knows my name
Where people don't fuss and fight, drink iced tea, and
dance on Saturday night
Where everyone likes country music and forgets everything
else
Watch Andy Griffith on TV and listen to Lawrence Welk.

I want to settle down in a one-horse town where everyone
knows my name
Where the city council meets in the country store and talks
about the baseball game.
I settled down in this little town; I thought this was the
place to be.
Times got bad; now I'm lonely and sad; all the people
moved away but me.

They'll come back to this little town where everyone
knows their names.
We'll pitch horseshoes, play checkers, and watch a baseball
game.
We'll sing and dance, drink iced tea 'til the break of dawn.
Our song for the town will be: "There's No Place Like
Home".

I REMEMBER

I remember Sen-Sen, Hoyts cologne and button shoes,
Warm Sunday afternoons and Monday morning blues;
Big wash tubs, black iron pots,
Wooden clothes pins and shoe laces with knots.

I remember the scent of fresh cut pine,
The bailing, sweet smell of syrup making time;
Yellow muskmelons and watermelon wine,
Eating the red right down to the rind.

I remember my mother's humor and the way my father
laughed,
The pretty brown cow and her baby calf;
The old hound dog, the pigs in the pen;
The big red rooster and the Dominique hen.

I remember sulfur and molasses Senna tea
And something tied in a rag called asafetida;
The warmth of the fire in the open fireplace,
And the red measles all over my face.

I can't go home again, that's for sure.
The memories grow more precious as I mature.
I could write a book of them, one at a time.
When I think of one, there is one close behind.

I'M GOING BACK TO DIXIE

I'm going back to Dixie with my wife on my knee.

We'll settle down in a small town and raise a family.
She'll do what the cookbook says on page number five,
And make big, country biscuits and sweet potato pie.

I'm going back to Dixie where the magnolias never die;
Where we stand and salute Old Glory on the Fourth of July;
And we cut the largest watermelon in the old melon patch;
And have a piece of pound cake that Mama made from
scratch.

I'm going back to Dixie where I was born and raised;
And buttermilk and corn bread was the best meal of the
day;
Where the family came together and the darkness settled in;
And we listened to the night sounds and the whisper of the
wind.

I'm going back to Dixie where Mama boils the okra, dumps
tomatoes in the pot,
And says, "We ain't got much for supper but thank God for
what we got."
Papa said the blessing. This is what he said,
"God bless America and please pass the corn bread."

IN THE COUNTRY

Mama's cooking cornbread, Papa's picking peas.
Dog's on the back porch, scratching at his fleas.
Chickens in the barnyard, scratching for a meal.
Cow needs milking, Papa's in the field.

The fields are white with cotton.
The corn is turning brown.
Got to get the harvest in
Before the snow starts coming down.
There is frost on the pumpkin;
The leaves are falling now.
I'll put away the working tools
There's nothing else to plow.

I must get a fire going;
There's a chill in the air.
Winter's just around the corner;
The trees are almost bare.

Mama's cooking cornbread.
The peas are in the pot.
The mules are in the stable.
The cows are in the lot.

Papa asked the blessing;
I bowed my weary head.
He asked God to bless America,
The black-eyed peas and cornbread.

MY FOUR CATS

My cats are my pride and joy;
Three girls and one boy.
My cats live within the law.
The only time they get a-lickin'
Is when they lick their paws.

Prissy naps all day;
Missy naps off and on.
T. T. tries to catch a nap;
Silvia won't leave him alone.

When I tell them what to do,
They act as if they can't hear.
They sit and look at me
As if to say, "We are the boss around here."

Prissy, the Mama, is a queen if there ever was one.
She doesn't think her job is done.
Night and day she stands guard
And lets every other cat know this is her back yard.

MY TOM CAT

When he came to live with us, he was just
a kitten;
He wasn't much larger than a baby's
mitten.
He was so young he could lick
The milk from my fingertips.

Soon he began to grow; he grew and grew
And everything was new.
He would play with a ball, a piece of
string, And get into everything.

We played hide-and-seek all over the house.
He would stay hidden as quiet as a mouse

Until I walked by, then he'd dart out
And wrap himself around my leg and hang on for dear life.

As he grew larger, he got tougher
And a little mean. I didn't like that.
I knew then that he wasn't a kitten anymore;
He is a big, red, tabby Tom Cat.

One day I saw a gleam in his eyes,
As he went and sat at the door.
I patted his head and let him out.
I wondered if I'd ever see him anymore.

He was gone for two or three days and when he returned,
His coat was be-draggled; he was tired, weary and thin.
I cleaned him up and gave him his supper
And tucked him in.

He has lived with us a long time now.
And when we can't go outside because of the weather,
He lays on the floor at my feet,
As I sit in my chair and we grow old together.

THE BEGINNING AND THE END
OF THE AMERICAN DREAM

I made an application for a G. I. loan
To buy one of those F. H. A. homes.
I asked the salesman how much the payments would be.
He said, "Oh, about two hundred and three."
I said, "Oh, me." The salesman calmed my fears

When he said, "You can pay it off in about thirty years.
If you get in a jam and your money runs out,
You don't have nothing to worry about.
We'll go along with ye."

I took my wife out to look at the house;
She screamed like she'd seen a mouse.
My knees trembled and I ran a temperature,
When she said, "We'll have to have some new furniture."
She said, "I'll go up town and look around."
Three truck loads were all she found.
She signed my name on the dotted line;
The salesman said, "Now that's just fine.
If you get in a jam and your money runs out,
You don't have nothing to worry about.
We'll go along with ye."

When we got settled down,
I cranked up my Chevvie and drove up town;
Looked around for a parking space;
Wound up down at the Cadillac place.

Two salesmen sitting in the shade
Said, "Hi there, buddy, wanta trade?"
I said, "Yeah, man."
He shook my hand
And said, "Take this cream puff and drive it around.
You can get this baby for six thousand and nothing down.
For a thousand more
You can get bucket seats and four in the floor,
Two carburetors, twin tail pipes,

Leather upholstery and back up lights."
I signed my name on the dotted line.
The salesman said, "Now that's just fine.
If you get in a jam and your money runs out,
You don't have nothing to worry about.
We'll go along with ye."

Then came the question of my old Belair;
The salesman said, "I want to be fair,
But it's hard to get rid of a used Belair."
He said, "I'll tell you what I'll do,
I'll give you fifty dollars and apply it on your loan
Or you can give me two fifty and take it back home."
I said, "What do you want me to do – lay it in your lap?"
Well, he said, "The engine's got a piston slap."
I said, "I just bought the tires last year."
He said, "The transmission's got a bad gear."
I said, "What about the seat covers – they're nearly new."
He said, "Take it or leave it,
I told you what I'd do."

The salesman looked like he was gonna have a stroke,
When I told him I'd take the Chevvie down and trade it for
a boat.
I drove in at the boat place;
The salesman stuck a paper in my face.
I signed my name on the dotted line.
The salesman said, "Now, that's just fine.
If you get in a jam and your money runs out,
You don't have nothing to worry about.
We'll go along with ye."

When the first of the month came rolling around
And I got the bills,
I lost twenty pounds
And began to have chills.
My wife said, "No use getting all upset
And worrying yourself dizzy.
Didn't they say they'd go along with ye?"
I said, "Well, I tried to tell them
But they wouldn't let me speak.
I don't have nothing to worry about,
I don't make but fifty dollars a week."

It wasn't long 'til the sheriff came around,
Said, "Come on, buddy, let's go up town."
We went up town to see the judge;
He said, "You can't get bail."
I said, "Well, how can I pay off these bills sitting in jail?
I'm no dead beat."
The judge wanted to know
If I could pay them a dollar a week.
"How long will that take?"
The judge said, "That depends on the interest rate.
I can make a guess,
About 70 years more or less."

They took the car, house and boat.
My credit's no good and we're broke.
We are living out of town in a ragged old tent.
Now they can't kick us out if we can't pay the rent.
It's like being in a boat paddling up stream,
The beginning and the end of the American dream.

THE OLD HOUSE BY THE SIDE OF THE ROAD

The old house by the side of the road,
No one lives there anymore.
There's the old hay barn and the old corn crib
And the smoke house with one hinge on the door.

There's the old cow pasture in front of the house.
The split rails have rotted away.
No cows in the pasture for me to go after
At the close of a long summer day.

The dinner bell is rusty on top of the pole.
I rang it many times as a lad.
The black walnut tree in the back yard
Was the only shade we had.

The old house by the side of the road
Stands lonely and forlorn.
The roof has fallen in;
The windows and doors are no more.

To the old house by the side of the road,
I'll say my last goodbye,
And take with me the memories
that make me laugh and cry.
I know I'll get homesick for the old home place
now and then.
The memories will remind me I can't go home again.

COTTON MILL WEAVE ROOM

I hear the shuttles slamming against the pickerstick,
Tuned to perfection; they never miss a lick.
Got the handles pulled toward me, hoping they won't stop.
It's money in my pocket, when there are picks on the clock.

I see the warpman coming; he knows what it's all about.
He's bringing a warp; I've got one running out.
I see the batteryfiller, working as she sings;
Bobbin by bobbin, she fills the magazines.

Some people like the music of all kinds of tunes.
I like the music in the slamming of the looms.
The rhythm is relaxing, just like a symphony.
When the shift is over, the sound will go with me.

There is nothing so satisfying,
As pulling handles on a loom,
And having a buddy along side
On the set in the weave room.

WE ARE PROUD TO CALL IT DIXIE

We are proud to call it Dixie
Where the summer breezes blow
And it's sunny every day.
We just take it easy in a lazy sort of way.

We are proud of the Mississippi
Where the river boats used to spin.
We still sing Swanee River
And read Huckleberry Finn.

We are proud to call it Dixie
And our hearts go out to you.
If you've never tasted our chicken
And our Hursey bar-b-que.

Come in and join us;
Sit awhile; take off your shoes;
Pass the time of day.
Just take it easy in a lazy sort of way.

We are proud to call it Dixie.
It has changed a bit for some.
We still take it easy
And say y'all come.

BACK HOME AGAIN

The magnolia trees are blooming. I smell the sweet
perfume.
A gentle breeze is blowing and I hear a country tune.
I see the fields of cotton and the corn so green and tall,
Way down south in Dixie where they say "you-all".

My rambling days are over. This is where my life began
Way down south in Dixie. Now I'm back home again

Together with my kinfolk. We'll dance and have a ball
Way down south in Dixie where they say "you-all".

The sights and sounds of Dixie bring back memories
Of corn bread and buttermilk and good ole black-eyed peas.
My rambling day are over. This is where my life began
Way down south in Dixie. Now I'm back home again.

I hear someone singing an old Gospel song.
The dinner bell is ringing, calling me home.
All around the table I see a smiling face,
Holding hands and praying, thanking God for his grace.

JUST A-SITTING AND A-WHITTLING

Just a-sitting and a-whittling on this old hickory stick,
Chewing my tobacco and a-spitting in the "crick".
Been doing some heavy thinking, got a lot on my mind.
I want to get it all done before supper time.

Pass the black-eyed peas and corn bread and some onions
down this way,
I've been doing some heavy thinking and I've had a hard
day.
I've got to get to bed early so I can get up at dawn.
I've got to do some heavy thinking after I put my thinking
cap on.

The sun is mighty bright this morning and my whittling
stick is smaller.
The "crick" is running faster and the trees are getting taller.

I've been thinking about that for nearly a week, while I was
a-sitting and A-whittling on this old hickory stick,
Chewing my tobacco and a-spitting in the "crick".

Just a-sitting and a-whittling on this old hickory stick,
Chewing my tobacco and a-spitting in the "crick".
I hear the birds a-singing and a dog barks now and then;
The crowing of a rooster and a cocking of a hen.

I had chicken for supper and while I was chewing on a leg,
I was thinking mighty heavy about which came first,
the chicken or the egg.
Been thinking about that for six weeks, just a-sitting and a-
whittling on This old hickory stick,
Chewing my tobacco and a-spitting in the "crick".

The sun is getting lower, my whittling is getting slower.
My whittling days are over 'cause the days are getting
colder.
I'll miss the sitting and the whittling on the old hickory
stick,
And chewing my tobacco and a-spitting in the "crick".

GOING BACK TO THE BLUE RIDGE

I'm going back to the Blue Ridge where there is peace and
quiet,
Away from the noise of the city and the sound of sirens day
and night;
Away from the fumes of pesticides and garbage dumps;
Away from the polluted rivers and the muddy swamps.

I want to be there when the moon comes up
And see the stars from peak to peak.
I want to hear the sounds of the mountains
And learn the language that they speak.

I want to roam the hills and valleys,
See the animals great and small.
I want to be there in the evening
When the twilight shadows fall.

I want to be there at sunset and watch the colors unfold;
A picture of so many colors the numbers are untold.
I want to feel the silence, hear the whisper of the wind.
I'm going back to the Blue Ridge; then I'll be home again.

HOW WE SURVIVED THE ICE STORM

The lights went out and the furnace stopped.
A limb snapped off like a pistol shot.
We are in trouble I thought, as my heart skipped a beat.
I wondered how we'd make it without any heat.

Marie said we can cook on the burner of the gas stove,
And turn on the oven when the room gets cold.
We made coffee and sat there and drank.
Marie said, "We've got hot water in the gas water tank."

When we calmed down, we began to get smart.
We went out and knocked the ice from the old Dodge Dart.
We took the ice and put it in the bath tub,
And that's the way we saved our grub.

Then we started worrying about the deep freeze stuff.
Marie said, "If we lose that it will sure be tough."
We have a pine tree and it sure looks sick,
With ice on the limbs about five inches thick.
The limbs are laying on a Duke Power line
And if they are not removed, it can break anytime.

The ice storm is over now and
I think of many times in the past,
When I have wondered how we would have ever made it
without PIEDMONT GAS.

A TIME FOR EVERYTHING UNDER THE SUN

A time to laugh, a time to cry;
A time to live, a time to die.

A time of sickness, a time to be well;
A time to seek Heaven, a time to avoid Hell.

A time to eat, a time to fast;
A time to be first, a time to be last.

A time to lose, a time to win;
A time to get out, a time to get in.

A time to walk, a time to run;
A time to be merry, a time to have fun.

A time to keep silent, a time to speak out;
A time to know what is a reasonable doubt.

A time to be angry, a time to be mad;
A time to remember the good times we had.

A time to be ashamed of our many sins;
A time to be sorry for the shape we're in.

A time to be still, a time to meditate;
A time to seek forgiveness before it's too late.

A time to lead, a time to be led;
A time for the people to bury the dead.

A time to till the soil, sow the seeds and hope for the best;
A time to do our part and wait for God to do the rest.

After all is said and done,
A time for everything under the sun.

A man's life is full of trouble; his days are few.
Here today and gone tomorrow, like the vapor from the dew.

I WOULDN'T TAKE A MILLION FOR MY MEMORIES

A thousand memories running through my mind,
Put them all together just to make a rhyme.
Wouldn't be enough of paper to write them all down.
They just keep coming and going wild and free.
I wouldn't give a nickel for my future,
And wouldn't take a million for my memories.

Memories of sunny days and cold winter nights,
The harvest moon in its flight,
Millions of stars from the mountains to the sea,
The feeling of freedom inside of me.
I wouldn't give a nickel for my future,
And wouldn't take a million for my memories.

Memories of twilight shadows creeping in,
The scent of honeysuckle and the whisper of the wind,
Night sounds and crickets make a melody
I'll forever cherish – My memories are a part of me.
I wouldn't give a nickel for my future,
And wouldn't take a million for my memories.

Acknowledgements

My sister had struggled in earnest for many years, and I in more recent years, with the persistent inner impulse – a calling to somehow share our Dad's many creative writings. This "mission" intensified becoming even more prominent. I spoke with Lisa Kobrin, Reference Librarian, at May Memorial Library in Burlington, N.C. Lisa suggested I explore local author books and there it was – THE BOOK *Life in the House by the Creek* by Charlie Wilson. This book of poems is about a youngster who was one of twelve children who grew up on a small truck farm near Burlington during the late 1940's and 1950's. I brought the book home and immediately read it from cover to cover – could not put it down. I knew at that moment somehow the "mission" could and would be accomplished – what a tremendous relief. This book had such an irresistible appeal and it became the pivotal inspiration, motivation and confidence builder that was needed to vigorously and seriously pursue our book of Dad's short stories and poems. Thank you, Charlie Wilson!

My sister and I are very appreciative of Wayne Drumheller's knowledge, encouragement and guidance enabling us to produce this collection of our Dad's writings. This being our first book, we were without direction and essentially overwhelmed. Wayne was a tremendous asset providing consultation and direct support relative to the creative, editing and publishing phases necessary to develop what we think is a quality work.

We want to extend our sincere gratitude to Pat Long of Elon, North Carolina for her patience, perseverance and willingness to prepare and organize the more than one hundred pages of manuscript and other material in a very professional form – something of a herculean task. Pat's background includes working as a legal secretary, secretary of the guidance department at Western Alamance High School and eventually retiring from Elon University after twenty years as a program assistant in Elon College, the College of Arts and Sciences. Knowing Pat had many years of experience and expertise in the legal and academic fields typing documents pertaining to each of those areas, she was the perfect person for the job. Pat's promptness of completing work allowed the project to move in a most timely, efficient and productive manner – a very smooth process. It was a joy to work with Pat and we are very thankful for her contribution to this book.

I have been utterly amazed by Judy Madren's work for more than thirty-five years. The moment I realized an illustrator would be essential to the book the first and only person I thought of was Judy Madren. I was truly elated when she agreed to take on the tasks of illustrating for the poems and short stories as well as designing the cover. She was able to provide illustrations that not only reinforced Dad's writing but gave them an enhanced depth and scope. Yes, a picture is worth a thousand words.

Judy's exceptional talent became the final perfect ingredient and we cannot thank her enough. As a young adult Judy studied under Florence Riddle and Betty Tyler, well-known local artists. Tyler's influence contributed heavily to Judy's development and an explosion of color, unique subject matter and the introduction of brushes along with the palette knife and application of oils in a free and unique manner. She has expanded her abilities in the use of pastels, colored pencils, acrylics and watercolor demonstrating her own unique style. Additionally, Judy has undertaken the mastery of watercolors utilizing the transparency technique under the tutelage of Carolyn Teague, an accomplished local watercolorist. Judy's works vary from realistic to abstract and impressionism. She gladly accepts commissions.

She is a member of the Burlington Artists League

Gallery, Alamance Arts and Alamance Artisans where her works can be viewed and purchased at each location.

Judy's talent has been recognized through many awards from various exhibits and shows to include best in Show, first, second, third places and honorable mention.

We offer our most sincere gratitude, beyond measure, to Dr. Sam Powell for his encouragement, support and endorsement of the book.

About the Editors and This book

Norma Green Heath

I was born in the textile community of Gaston County, North Carolina and I have resided in Burlington, North Carolina since 1943. After graduating from Walter Williams High School I was married to Paul Ray Heath for fifty-six years until his passing in 2015. I was employed for thirty-two years by the United States Department of Defense as an industrial specialist located at the Western electric plant in Burlington before retiring in 1993.

Central to my life is Kinnett Memorial Baptist church where I faithfully attend services and participate regularly in senior and other activities. I have a daughter Cynthia McKissick Cash and two grandchildren Graison Heath McKissick and Christiana Abigail Cash.

Tim Green

I was born and reared in Burlington, North Carolina. After graduating from Walter Williams High School and Elon College, I served four years in the U.S. Air Force during the Vietnam Era. I earned a master's degree in Public Administration from The University of North Carolina at Greensboro.

I consider myself very fortunate to have held for ten years the position of assistant area director of The Alamance-Caswell Area Mental Health, Mental Retardation and Substance Abuse Program. I appreciate the many opportunities given to me by director John Moon to develop in that capacity. Subsequently, I was privileged and honored to serve for more than twenty years as director of The Alamance County Health Department. Serving as president of The North Carolina Association of Local Health Directors and receiving the prestigious Dr. Ham Stevens Award for Outstanding Leadership and the North Carolina Public Health Association's Reynolds Award were some highlights of my career.

Since retiring in 2005, I was interim health director in Person and Chatham Counties and led teams that accredited local health departments in more than thirty-five counties in North Carolina. I thoroughly enjoyed my class room work with Elon University seniors as a part-time instructor. More recently family ancestry has been a special interest.

I am a proud, active member of the Alamance Battleground Chapter of The National Society of Sons of the American Revolution. Words fall woefully short in my attempts to describe the unbridled enthusiasm and satisfaction to see Dad's work now available in book form.

My wife Dawn and I live in Graham, North Carolina.

tdgreen02@bellsouth.net

Wave Goodbye at the Corner

Made in the USA
Columbia, SC
24 June 2019